TABLE OF CONTENTS

The X-Mas Files

CLASSIFIED Secrets From the North Pole

I'll admit it. I used to believe in Santa and all that Christmas magic. But I've since come to discover the truth. So I'll just come out and say it. You were lied to.

Everything you've been told about Christmas and the magic of the holiday is part of a conspiracy that stretches as wide as Santa's belly and as long as his beard.[1] Because the truth about Santa? You may think you know the tale of ol' Saint Nick, the one they call Kris Kringle, the "giving soul" known as Father Christmas. But let me break it to you . . . you don't know the man. I mean, listen, if this was a trustworthy guy, why would he have so many different names? That seems like a man hiding something.

INSIGHT
KIDS

SAN RAFAEL • LOS ANGELES • LONDON

[1] His beard of lies!

My name is Elmer and I am an elf. (See, one name. Just sayin'.) I live and work at the North Pole, crafting toys tirelessly under Santa's watchful, twinkling eye. I am writing to you, children of the world, to debunk the magic of Christmas. I will pull back the tinsel-covered curtain on the truth about what happens up North, where the elves, the reindeer, and pretty much everyone but Santa himself work all day.

In this book, you'll be introduced to Santa's disgruntled brother-in-law, Hank, who runs the Mall Santa scam. You'll read about the grumpy, ankle-biting pet penguin that ol' Claus lets run free. You'll discover the existence of South Pole elves, who have waged an endless battle against Santa and his North Pole elves that began with harmless snowball fights and has led to war crimes such as replacing all of our candy canes, gumdrops, and lollipops with . . . sugar-free breath mints.

Let's start with *this*. When *you* go to school, does your teacher assign you a nickname and force you to go by it for the rest of the year? No, of course not. That would be weird. But in Santa's kingdom, the weirdness is real. Santa is so eccentric, that every year, he initiates the new elves with a peculiar ceremony he calls . . .

THE SAINT NICK-NAMING CELEBRATION

As every newly recruited elf enters, they are brought before the assembly of elves and given a metallic disc known as a cymbal. Santa lets out a sudden, bellowing scream, which forces the stunned elf to *drop* the cymbal. Saint Nick then nicknames elves based on the sound the cymbal makes as it clatters to the floor. My best friend is named *Clank*.

His brother is *Smash*. The gal who lives a few doors down is *Berrrrrrang* and her roommate is *Tink-tonk-donk*.

If that wasn't bad enough, Santa doesn't let us use our last names. *Those* are determined by your favorite crayon color, which is perfectly fine for *Smack Indigo*, which has a bit of a rock-star vibe, but not as good for *Splat Brown* . . . which was my nickname.

But here I am, reclaiming the elf I once was. I am Elmer Elffenstock . . . and I am here to expose the truth.

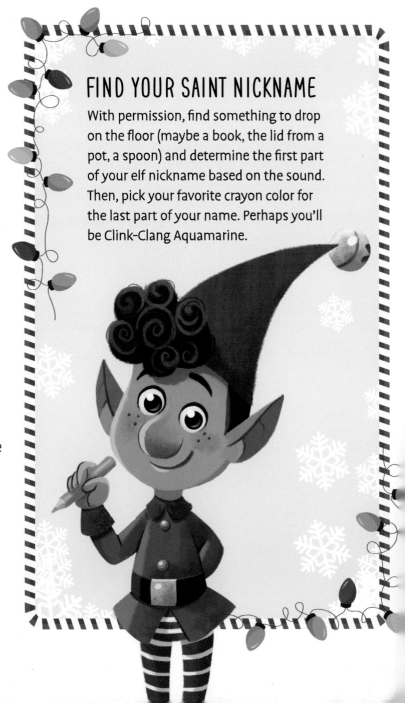

FIND YOUR SAINT NICKNAME

With permission, find something to drop on the floor (maybe a book, the lid from a pot, a spoon) and determine the first part of your elf nickname based on the sound. Then, pick your favorite crayon color for the last part of your name. Perhaps you'll be Clink-Clang Aquamarine.

Some think of Saint Nick as a jolly old gentleman with the patience of . . . well, a saint. A grandfatherly figure who spends his days reading letters written by hopeful children, much like yourself. He puts on his spectacles, carefully opens each envelope, and proceeds to read each handwritten word with great care. "*Dear Santa,*" the children write, "*This year for Christmas I want a new bike, a cute puppy, a trampoline that's bigger than the neighbor's across the street,*" blah blah blah.

This one may sting, but the truth is . . . Santa employs Screener Elves.

What is a Screener Elf, you ask? Well, you see, Santa considers himself to be the kingpin. Sort of like the Snow-ny Soprano of the North. You know what I'm saying? No? All right, well, basically, Santa would never allow just any old letter to make it to his desk. The Screener Elf Squad was formed thanks to the December long ago when Santa's estranged brother-in-law, Hank,

sent him mail disguised as a letter from some sweet kid named Frank that triggered a stink bomb when it was opened. That was just the beginning. Over the years, Santa's added to the screeners' list. For instance, he has his elves screen all letters to make sure that the children who wrote them didn't have grubby hands. A little smear of peanut butter may seem perfectly harmless to a kid, but Santa takes soiled correspondence *very* seriously.

Recently, Santa has begun to put a heavier workload on his Screener Elves' shoulders. "I'm busy!" he'll bellow as a Screener Elf, arms straining with the weight of a thousand approved letters, stands at his door. "I've got a ho-ho-whole lotta stuff to do, so why don't you take care of all those?"

And just this year, Santa released an updated memo to the Screener Elves.

MEMO

From the Desk of Santa Claus
Date: December 2

To all Screener Elves,

From this day forward, letters to Santa **MUST** contain the following key words and phrases:

- The phrase "pretty please" at least three times

- The word "flibberty jibberty"

- Any combination of the adjectives "well-dressed," "majestic," "awe-inspiring," and "strapping" when referring to me

- The phrase "free dessert"

Letters to Santa **MUST NOT** contain the following key words and phrases:

- The phrases "I need," "I want," or "I demand"

- Words that rhyme with "Hank," "south," "flan," or "underwear"

- Misspelled words

Furthermore, letters with the following misspelled words **WiLL NOT** only be disqualified but shall be thrown into the spam bin and used as kindling for the annual post-Christmas bonfire:

"**Claws**," "**freind**," "**sinserly**," "**mery**," "**cristmas**."

LETTER TO SANTA

Can you make it past Santa's Screener Elves? Draft a letter to ol' Saint Nick using all of Santa's key words and phrases and none of the disqualifying ones.

Hint: Addressing your letter to Tamoshantamis Pinkleclaushensteen will automatically move your letter to the top of Santa's pile (see December 21).

_____

_____

_____

_____

_____

By now, you may think that I'm just a disgruntled elf spreading lies about Santa Claus. Perhaps I was denied a promotion. Maybe Santa laughed a little too hard when "Splat Brown" was decided as my nickname. I'll tell you this, though. I'm not the only one who has had it up to here (imagine me gesturing as high as possible, but then picture it *way* higher because . . . well, you know—I'm an elf) with Santa's antics. So I will tell you the tale of Speeeerang Sepia . . . the elf that went rogue.

Speeeerang Sepia was part of the crew of elves in charge of the Naughty or Nice List. They would assess the Shelf Elf reports on each child and were tasked with stamping the child's file with one of their two big rubber stamps. If the child was good—BAM! The elves would stamp their file with a big red blocky "NICE." But if the child had spent the year acting like a nincompoop, disrespecting their elders, watching low-quality TV, or using words that I dare not repeat . . . the *other* stamp came out.

One Christmas season not too long ago, Speeeerang Sepia was feeling massively overworked. The Naughty or Nice Squad had been given data at the last possible minute and were scrambling to catch up. It may have been the pressure of the work.

It may have been the relentless BAM! BAM! BAM! of the rubber stamps slamming on the files, over and over again. We don't know what caused it. All we know was that Speeeerang Sepia had finally reached her breaking point. She hopped up on top of her files and, holding a freshly inked NAUGHTY stamp, let out a yowling battle cry. She STAMPED the elf to her left: NAUGHTY! She STAMPED the elf to her right: NAUGHTY! She STAMPED the elf trying to wrestle the stamp away from her: NAUGHTY!

Speeeerang continued her rampage . . . er, *stampage*, until she was finally stopped and pushed off to coal duties. The lesson remains, though . . . the Naughty or Nice List? Not exactly reliable.

NAUGHTY OR NICE CHALLENGE

Since you now know how overworked the Naughty or Nice Crew can be, why don't *you* determine who has been Naughty and who has been Nice? All you need are two big cups or bowls: one labeled "Naughty" and the other labeled "Nice." Then, gather 10 items small enough to be tossed into the cups. Coins, ping-pong balls, or even marshmallows would do the trick. Pick up an item, take two big steps back, and aim for the cups. After you do this with all 10 items, count how many of them landed in each cup. Whichever cup has more items in it is the list that you've made!

By now, you may be thinking that the North Pole elves are a real joke. And sure, while I don't always get along with my fellow elves, I can say this about them. They *aren't* the biggest slackers at the North Pole. The reindeer are.

The elves are divided into squads that take on all of the various tasks leading up to Christmas. You know about the Screener Elves and the Naughty or Nice Elves, and I'm sure you've heard of the toy makers, but there are more elf jobs than you could possibly imagine. And while we elves work ourselves into a frenzy worthy of Speeeerang Sepia herself, Santa's reindeer frolic about without a care in the world. Doing what? Playing their little reindeer games.

From Dasher, to Dancer, to Prancer, to that one with the red nose whose name I can never remember, the reindeer spend the entire season goofing off. While we are hard at work, they're getting those knobby knees all tangled up playing party games like Twister: Reindeer Edition. They're gathering at the Games Stadium, facing off in the Snow Volleyball Tournament. They're breaking into the toy-making workshop every time Bonk Green the Security Elf falls asleep. They're even distracting the most patient of us all, the Shelf Elves, by baiting those professional sitters into games of Hide & Seek! One of the biggest pitfalls of playing Hide & Seek with the reindeer is that while you might not easily find *them*, you'll certainly have no problem finding their poops.

So the next time you feel sorry for those poor dears who have to lug Santa and his sack of gifts around for one night of the year, just talk to the hand.

REINDEER GAMES

Reindeer are known for their lollygagging and all those silly games, it's true. But the elves only really ever complain when they're assigned scoop duties (or should I say scoop doodies?). That's right, it's a dirty job, but some elf's gotta do it. So why not pretend you're an elf and play a reindeer game of your own? Grab a spoon, a container, and head out to the icy tundra (aka yard or any large outdoor space) to see who can scoop up the most reindeer poop!

To set up this game, the first step is scattering the "poop." Reindeer poop tends to have an oddly sweet smell because they eat nothing but Mrs. Claus's cookies, so chocolate puff cereal or marshmallows make excellent reindeer droppings. Set a timer for three minutes. The elves then race around, scooping up "poop" and carrying it back to their containers. The elf who's collected the most poops after three minutes is the winner of this reindeer game!

One of the main questions that elves are asked is if we live at the North Pole or do we just work there. As much as I'd like to say that I live a couple of blocks away, enjoying the fruits of my hard labor in a two-bedroom, two-bath townhouse with a Jacuzzi tub, walk-in closet, and state-of-the-art kitchen, the truth is that I live in the Elf Dorms. That's right, they're exactly like college dormitories, except the ceilings are much lower.

Each Elf Dorm houses three roommates, which isn't too bad considering the size of the rooms. But the way that Santa decides who rooms with who is a bit . . . curious. The only question that seemed a bit strange was that last one, and all three of us roommates chose the number 1. We now live in the only room in the entire Elf Dorm that's right between the men's and ladies' room. What's up with that?

Fill out the Elf Dorm questionnaire with your family and friends and see how many answers match up. Who would be your roommate?

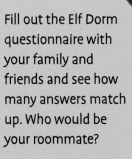

ELF DORM APPLICATION QUESTIONNAIRE

Elf Nickname: _____

TRUE OR FALSE: The fact that some stuffed animals are taller than you makes you feel like less of an elf. TRUE _____ FALSE _____

WOULD YOU RATHER have to loudly sing the chorus of "Jingle Bells" every time you walk into a room for a week

OR . . . have to wear a Santa suit every day for a week?

WOULD YOU RATHER only eat fruitcake for five days

OR . . . only eat candy canes for five days?

WOULD YOU RATHER have a nose that glows red[1]

OR . . . have pointy elf ears?[2]

WOULD YOU RATHER win the lottery

OR . . . grow to reach a normal height?

PROBLEM SOLVING: You have to get a gift off of the top shelf, which is obviously far out of your reach. You only have three items: a candy cane, a piece of thread, and a puffy sticker. How do you get the gift?

_____
_____
_____
_____

RANK: On a scale from 1 to 10, rank how okay you are with living next to the bathroom?

1 2 3 4 5 6 7 8 9 10

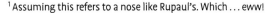

[1] Assuming this refers to a nose like Rupaul's. Which . . . eww!

[2] This particular question had me bumfuzzled and seemed particularly, well, pointless since we elves take great pride in our pointy ears.

Ah, Christmas magic. Santa makes it all look so easy, delivering gifts to bajillions of houses throughout the world in a single night! He, as a well-fed gentleman, manages to slide down the slimmest of chimneys. He even manages deliveries to places with zero chimneys all on account of his sparkly holiday hocus-pocus . . .

Well, I'm here to tell you that it's all a bunch of malarkey!

What *you* see as Christmas magic really comes down to teamwork and some serious MacGyver-ing on the part of ol' Claus's reindeer crew. I know. I had a lot to say about those rowdy reindeer a couple days ago, but the truth is that nine-tenths of Christmas magic is actually reindeer trickery. What I'm about to tell you isn't exactly *legal*, though, so let's keep this on the down low, okay? Here's how Santa and his gaggle of reindeer handle their break-ins.

Dasher is in charge of the speed. As the resident reindeer mechanic, he has fitted each of the A-Team reindeer with jet fuel–powered skates that allow them to literally dash from roof to roof in record time.

Dancer is in charge of distraction. If a kid wakes up as Santa is squeezing down the chimney, Dancer will take charge of the situation. She got her name from the way she used to catch a child's attention through the bedroom window, distracting them with an elaborate tap dance complete with top hat and cane. But after years of performing, Dancer has gotten lazy. Now, she creeps over to the window and utters a loud whinny, causing the child to scurry back to bed so Santa can complete his hit.

Prancer and Vixen have the responsibility of handling the situation in which the chimney isn't . . . let's just say

Santa-friendly in size. Generally, they're able to squeeze Santa down the chimney with the combo of a tummy-restricting girdle borrowed from Mrs. Claus, some duct tape, a vat of special Slippery Santa Jelly, and a powerful push. When this doesn't work though . . .

Cupid comes into play. Cupid was doing hard-time crimes including zoo break-ins and more when Santa recruited him. Cupid, you see, has turned his antlers into a set of handy Swiss Army–like gadgets that can open doors, unlatch windows, and break into anything, be it a house, a car, or, obviously, a zoo. Freed from the zoo on Cupid's most infamous crime spree were Donner and Blitzen, who are now Cupid's right- and left-hand reindeer. In the event that Cupid's antlers can't get Santa into a home, Donner uses brute force to break in, after which, Blitzen, a handy repair reindeer, fixes the damage before anyone can notice.

And what was the other one? I can never remember his name. Randall, I think. He used to provide flashlight services, but now he tends to spend Christmas Eve bragging about his glory days.

ANTLER ART

Using arts and crafts supplies such as pipe cleaners, wire, tape, scissors, stickers, and glue, make your own special set of reindeer antlers that can act as a back scratcher, a dog petter, or perform functions like picking up the TV remote or holding a pen and writing a note with it.

What if I told you that there is a secret squad of elves called the Adjustors that really do know if you've been getting up to some last-minute Naughty activities?

You see, once the Naughty and Nice List is processed, things are pretty much set in stone. Each column of children is assigned gifts based on their official N-N Rating. For example, if someone has an 88/42 N-N Rating, they've racked up far more Naughty points than Nice. So rather than getting the number one item on their wish list, they'll get the toy that they rolled their eyes at while shopping a few months ago. Out with the PlayStation, in with the doll with one eye stuck shut and a malfunctioning sound chip that once said, "Feed me" but now just says "Beef."

There is a possibility, though, of Naughty activity after the N-N Ratings are processed. That's where the Adjustors come in.

Adjustor Elves are deployed along with Santa on Christmas Eve to patrol the houses of children that have been deemed "questionable" by the Shelf Elves . . . and we'll get to those tricky little bad boys later. Adjustors are special ops elves that visit the homes of these Questionable Kids mere hours before the gifts are set to be opened, watching for the ones who dare to sneak out of bed to take a peek inside one of their presents.

And if they do?

The Adjustor, who has been trained to perfectly replicate the yawns of parents, will yawn loudly, causing the QK to flee from the gift in fear of getting caught in the act of peekery. Once the QK is back in bed, the Adjustor strikes. And with a snap of their finger, one of the presents disappears.

Such is the way of Santa.

Personally, me? I'd let a kid take a peek. Knowing the truth never hurt anyone, which is why I continue to tell my tale.

PEEK & FIND

Can you find the Adjustor Elf ready to snap your present away for being . . . questionable? As you search, try and spot these additional objects in the scene:

Oh, the joys of Christmas traditions. Decorating the tree with tinsel, ornaments, and lights, baking Christmas cookies, building gingerbread houses, and waking one morning to find the thing that you've waited all year for . . . the Elf on the Shelf.

As part of Santa's most elaborate scheme, the skinniest, scrawniest elves from the Naughty or Nice Squad shed their uniforms to don the standard-issue red onesies, apply false lashes and bronzer, climb into little cardboard boxes, and are deployed to homes around the world in order to spy on little children.

Yup, the Shelf Elf is a scout for ol' Santa, watching your behavior 24/7. Did you take a couple more cookies than your parents said you could have? Did you make a mess and blame it on your pet? Did you get a bad report card, dissolve it in a bath of water and chemicals to destroy the evidence, flush the remaining pulp away, and then tell your parents that it never came? Well, your Shelf Elf saw you, and as soon as you fall asleep, he'll fly back to the North Pole to submit his report to the Big Man in Red. Right?

Wrong. Flying is not in the Shelf Elf's job description. Yes, their N-N reports are delivered to Santa every night, but not in person. They're delivered via text.

The truth is that those little shelf-sitters have the cushiest job out of all the elves. They have just three simple tasks to do all day. Number one: do not move. Number two: text Santa a list of all the good things and bad things you've done that day. And number three? While everyone's sound asleep and dreaming, he's terribly, horribly busy . . . finding a new shelf.

Okay, originally, the elf spies actually *did* fly back and forth every night to deliver their N-N reports. But that all changed years ago when a certain Naughty or Nice Elf was promoted to Shelf Elf. His name was Doink Scarlet.

Doink was notoriously lazy, and prided himself on getting out of all duties that involved physical exercise of any kind. Also, he had a bad hip. So when he was deployed to the Dirkendorf family as a Shelf Elf, he thought he'd won the lottery. But after just one day on the shelf and one round trip to and from the North Pole, Doink was exhausted and had had enough. He hid himself in a dusty old Amazon box in the Dirkendorfs' attic and was never seen or heard from again.

SHELF ELF EVALUATION

Would you be a good Scout Elf? Take the following test and have a friend or family member decide if you make the cut:

 On a scale from 1 to 10, how lazy are you?

 True or False? You enjoy wearing onesies and fake eyelashes are your thing.

 Can you sit still with a blank expression on your face for two entire minutes? Try it now!

 Are you a good liar . . . er, actor? Let's put that to the test. Here is the scenario. You are a Shelf Elf and the child you've been spying on has just caught you texting. Play out the scene to convince the child that they're just imagining things. Go!

Now, I'm sure many of you wonder what role Santa's wife, Kitty, plays in all of the holiday hullabaloo. Well, for one, she does all the menu planning at the North Pole. She's also on the judging panel of the Ugly Christmas Sweater Pageant (more on this later). But the most intriguing thing I can tell you about Kitty Claus is that she invented gift wrapping.

If you can believe it, gifts used to be left under Christmas trees without a shred of wrapping paper covering them. Every Christmas morning, excited children would burst from their rooms, smiling from ear to ear, racing to the Christmas tree . . . and with one glance at the gifts, Christmas was over. There was no anticipation, no surprise.

Kitty, having noticed how Christmas morning magic just wasn't living up to the hype anymore, decided to fix things. She developed a process of wrapping colorful sheets of paper around a gift and gluing the paper sheets in place. Over the years, individual sheets of paper became long rolls of it, clear tape replaced the glue, ribbons and shiny bows were added to the process, and a line of stick-on labels was developed, taking the guesswork out of handing out similar-shaped presents. Genius, right?

But believe it or not, this wasn't Kitty's first attempt at making Christmas gift giving more exciting. Her first idea . . . was a real bust.

Kitty Claus's initial idea was to station an elf at every single Christmas tree worldwide. When the children awoke and ran toward the tree, said elf would engage them in a wrestling match. Only when the kid had wrestled the elf to the ground would they be able to open their gifts. Kitty had high hopes that the tradition would catch on, but it instead led to thousands of elf-injuries and stacks and stacks of hospital bills.

So the following year, Kitty settled on the idea of gift wrapping, including the 100 percent peek-proof present wrap, while those elves tasked with wrestling children, formerly known as the WWE (Worldwide Wrestling Elves), have since become the Adjustors. This has limited, but not totally erased, the amount of elf-injuries reported annually.

WRAPPIN' WITH MRS. CLAUS

Can you wrap a peek-proof present with minimal resources? Wrap a small present using the following: a sheet of paper, plastic wrap, and three pieces of tape. Then give the present to a friend or family member to try and unwrap to see how peek-proof it really is!

THE DAY: DECEMBER 10

It isn't only Santa who makes the experience at the North Pole a bizarre one. You see, while children spend the month of December preparing for the arrival of Christmas Day, we elves prepare for war.

Well, not so much *war* as a series of endless pranks between North Pole elves and South Pole elves, but you get the picture. The bitter rivalry between these two factions of elves comes down to this: *We're the North Pole elves and we're in charge of Christmas. YAY! We're the South Pole elves and we're in charge of . . . not Christmas! BOOOO!*

Now, what makes us North Pole elves special? Nothing, really. It's where we were born. Santa runs the North Pole while his brother-in-law Hank runs the South Pole. The North Pole elves handle Christmas, while the South Pole elves are stuck with making greeting cards for all the *other* holidays. Sure, it can be fun to create Saint Patrick's Day cards, covered with shamrocks, pots o' gold, and strange little leprechauns dressed in green. But when your job is making "Hooray for May Day" cards or ones that declare "Happy Administrative Professionals' Day," it can really crush an elf's soul!

I imagine, that is. I have no idea, personally. I'm a North Pole elf, born and raised. North Side!

Every year, on December 10, a faction of North Pole elves head south to unleash Santa's forces on our rivals. One year, we wrapped the entire South Pole in candy cane–striped toilet paper. Another time, we arrived in a huge chocolate statue of Hank that appeared to be a peace offering from Santa. Overnight, we nibbled our way out of the chocolate and switched all of the greeting cards with signed portraits of Santa.

You may be asking yourself, "Why would the North Pole elves, who have *everything*, target the South Pole?"

Because they have infiltrated our ranks.

MAKE-A-CARD

What is the next occasion you will be celebrating after Christmas? Is there a birthday coming up in your family? Do you exchange Valentine's Day cards with your friends? Make like a South Pole elf and create a personalized card for this next special occasion.

So here's a question I bet you're dying to ask. Who are all those other guys dressed like Santa that you see at shopping malls? Some of them do look a bit like Santa Claus, with oversized bellies and crinkly eyes. They may even bellow out a convincing "HO HO HO!" that echoes through the halls of the mall. But ask yourself this: Why does Santa's freakishly tall elf look a lot like a bored teenager texting on his phone? And the lady with the name tag that says Mrs. Claus . . . didn't you see her last week working at Pretzel Plaza in the food court?

The Mall Santa thing is an elaborate business run by Hank and the South Pole elves. In order to make a buck on his rival's name, ol' Southie Hank hires an army of Santas, supplying his counterfeit Clauses with fake beards, red suits, and pillowy bellies.

SUIT UP

Create your own fake Santa costume using materials like construction paper and cotton balls for your beard, a pillow stuffed under a big red shirt for your belly, black shoes or boots, a red hat, white gloves, etc. Then practice shouting things like "HO HO HO!" "Merrrrrry Christmas!" or "Happy Hankmas!" until you're ready for duty!

These trick Saint Nicks are deployed to malls everywhere to listen to the wishes of children so that Hank can collect data on what children really want. While Santa himself is busy with activities like the Ugly Christmas Sweater Pageant (see December 18), Hank is gathering info about kids and their wishes so he can one day one-up Santa with his own holiday. Hank's holiday, to take place on December 26, will be even more beloved than Christmas, and will be known as . . . Hankmas.

Now, before we move on from the epic rivalry between North and South Pole elves, I'm going to tell you a secret. I have proof that there are traitors in our ranks. We have been infiltrated by the South Pole elves.

While *we* stick to the annual Prank-a-Palooza on the tenth, those South Pole nincompoops prank us throughout the month of December. They regularly send double agents over to attack us from the inside, posing as North Pole elves looking for work.

For example, an elf who lived down the hall from me, BOOM Lavender, was eventually outed as a South Pole elf. I thought BOOM was a nice, quiet guy. I even gave him the occasional fist bump when we crossed paths. Which happened a lot, because he is a *big* coffee drinker and I live next to the bathroom. Anyway, BOOM Lavender was

revealed to be a South Pole infiltrator when he got caught red-handed putting stink bombs into the gifts of kids on the Nice List. He was apprehended and, when questioned, confessed his undying devotion . . . to Hank.

It turns out that BOOM Lavender was actually the notorious South Pole elf known as Atlanta Claus.

That's another reason Santa spends resources pranking Hank and his South Pole elves. You see, unlike the nicknames Santa gives us based on cymbal sounds and favorite colors, Hank gives his elves nicknames that poke fun at Santa. Besides Atlanta Claus, there's Piñata Claus, Havana Claus, and even Banana Claus, not to mention Santa Jaws, Saint Thick, Ain't Nick, Kris Dingle, Grandfather Clause, and so on.

The war of pranks between poles, it seems, will never end.

NAME THAT ELF

Can you match the South Pole elves to their nicknames based on what you know about Hank and his nicknaming pranks?

A

B

C

So you know by now that not all elves are toy makers. You know about the Adjustor Elves, who snatch presents away from peeking kids. You've heard of the Naughty or Nice Elves who wield the mighty rubber stamp. However, elves have all different kinds of responsibilities that would boggle your mind.

There's the Christmas Spirit Squad, a group of scientist elves who use a complicated system of thermometers, spy cameras, and listening devices to monitor the amount of Christmas cheer in the world.

There's the Kitchen Squad, led by Kitty Claus, which handles food for the other elves and the reindeer, but mostly for Santa. They are required to cater to Santa's every whim. If he's in a Baja shrimp taco kind of mood, time to roll out the tortillas. If he's recently watched an episode of *Chopped*, the Kitchen Squad competes to make meals out of mystery basket ingredients like buttermilk, chicken feet, and chocolate-covered ants. If it's less than two weeks till the big day and Santa doesn't fit into his suit, we *all* find ourselves on a week-long diet of kale, baby carrots, and puffed rice cakes.

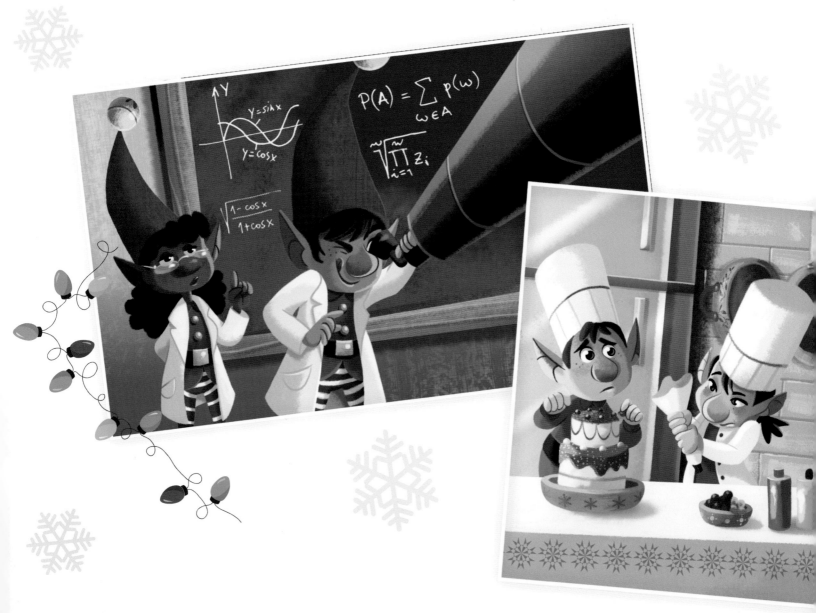

[1] The insufferable Ping-a-Ding Peach has been the Right-Hand Elf for 13 years in a row now. Here I am, working my bottom off serving on multiple elf squads, and Ping-a-Ding has it easy calling the shots for the Toy-Making Squad.

Then there is the Reindeer Training Squad, which is one step above the Coal Patrol (see December 22) and involves pretty much the same exact amount of shoveling.

And finally, there is the Scout Elf Squad (aka the Shelf Elf Squad).

Santa assesses each squad of elves every year, monitoring which elves are hitting their quotas. On the rare occasion that an elf hits their staggeringly high quota every day for seven years in a row, they become Santa's Right-Hand Elf for a year,[1] which essentially means they get to boss the rest of us around. Somehow, the winner always ends up being a toy maker. Hitting a toy-making quota, you see, is a lot less spirit-crushing than hitting a poop-scooping quota over at the Reindeer Training Squad.

SANTA SAYS

Take turns being Santa and acting out the commands in this Christmas version of Simon Says. Act out each elf task, but only if Santa Says!

Santa says . . . scoop the reindeer poop!

Santa says . . . whip me up some chicken and waffles!

Hand me the NAUGHTY stamp!

If you act only when Santa says, you win and get promoted to Right-Hand Elf for the day. But if you lose, it's off to reindeer poop-scooping duty for you.

THE DAY: DECEMBER 14

One of the most common questions we get in our letters to Santa is how the man fits all of those toys in his sack. Now, that's the kind of question that *some* elves would consider nosy and BOOM—they'd hit it with a NAUGHTY stamp right then and there. But not me. I understand the inquisitive mind. I have questions myself.

Here's how it happens.

Santa and his reindeer squad hit the rooftops, and you already know how they do that. They've got the girdle and the jelly ready, and Cupid and his two helpers are on deck ready to pull off a successful break-in. Are the elves done, though? Does their job conclude once the gifts are out for delivery?

Of course not! An elf's work is never done.

While Santa goes from rooftop to rooftop with his mammalian squad, elves from the Flight Squad operate gift-bearing drones above him. There are drones assigned

to every neighborhood and, once Santa wraps up a neighborhood, he lets out a mighty "HO HO HO!" which many assume to be his jolly laugh. In actuality, it's a code word. "HO" stands for "HOLDIN' OPEN," which is the signal for the pilot elves to drop their loads into Santa's now-empty sack. So what you think of as Christmas magic is actually a combo of communication and precision drone flight at work.

SANTA'S BAG OF TRICKS

How many gifts can you fit into Santa's Bag? Grab a pillowcase and an assortment of soft, squishy items such as clothing, stuffed animals, and soft toys. Then hold the pillowcase open (be sure to shout "Holdin' Open!") and have a friend or family member toss items to you to catch. Take turns tossing and catching to see who can fit the most items into Santa's Bag!

THE DAY: DECEMBER 15

The attentive reader may remember my reference to the "ankle-biting penguin" in the first chapter. Now, listen. I don't judge. Plenty of people (not me, but other people) love pets. But every kind of pet comes with its challenges, am I right? There are dog people, and while pups can be cute and cuddly, those things are basically furry, panting slobber machines. There are cat people, but if you don't trim a cat's nails, you could end up with an arm looking a bit like a candy cane. There are even bird people, and while it might be fun to teach a bird to say something worthy of a NAUGHTY stamp, that constant squawking can wear on an elf's ears. All of those things I can accept.

But what if I told you that Santa's beloved animal was essentially a waddling pair of scissors? I'm talking about Noel, Santa's pet penguin.

First of all, while it's nice to have someone shorter than *me* around the North Pole, why does a penguin get a name as nice as Noel and here I am with the name Splat?

Second of all, Santa told us he was getting a pet when he took us all on a field trip to Antarctica,[1] but I've since figured out the truth. My first hint came to me one wintery morning. As I was clearing the freshly fallen snow from the path between the Elf Dorms and the Christmas Spirit Observatory, I waved to Noel, who simply stared back at me with beady eyes. Beady, empty, black eyes.

Then, it lunged.

Ever since, Noel makes a beeline for me every time it sees me. I complained to Santa, who just told me that Noel has a "playful spirit," but I know better.

Noel . . . is an attack penguin.

Santa spent hours on our Antarctica trip mulling over which of the penguins to pick. There were cuter penguins. There were pudgier penguins prime for cuddles. But what Santa was looking for, I believe, was the sharpest beak.

This may sound like a conspiracy theory, but I believe Noel the Attack Penguin isn't a pet . . . it's a guard hired to protect the North Pole from South Pole infiltrators.

Why Noel would attack *me*, though, I cannot imagine.

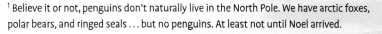

---

[1] Believe it or not, penguins don't naturally live in the North Pole. We have arctic foxes, polar bears, and ringed seals . . . but no penguins. At least not until Noel arrived.

Starting at the Reindeer Stables, help Splat make
his way along the trail to get to the Elf Dormitories
avoiding the obstacles ... and Noel ... along the way!

REINDEER
STABLES

SPLAT'S
DORM

Things can get pretty stressful at the North Pole during peak toy-making season. As the Naughty or Nice List is finalized and the last gifts are wrapped, every Toy Maker Elf has a quota of one thousand toys per day. This is the *one* time of the year where the Toy-Making Squad has it as hard as the rest of us. During this hectic time, the toy makers often have to pull elves from different squads to replace elves who have collapsed from the stress.

This time can be so stressful that *some* elves resort to trickery. Recently, I've witnessed elves creating snowy duplicates of themselves and positioning them at their workstations. That way, if Santa or his Right-Hand Elf (most likely Ping-a-Ding Peach) peeks into the workshop to check up on things, they will see what appears to be an elf, hard at work. Meanwhile, the *actual* elf is elsewhere, enjoying a hot mug of cocoa and a much-needed break.

TOY MAKERS WORKSHOP

This can backfire, though. One time, a Toy Maker Elf named Ka-BANG Cornflower constructed an incredibly realistic snow clone of himself. He even used food coloring and a set of sculpting tools to get his exact features correct. It looked so realistic that, when another elf bumped into it and knocked its head off, three of Ka-BANG's co-workers fainted out of shock.

BUILD-A-CLONE

If it's snowy where you live, head outside and build a snow clone of yourself. Pay careful attention to details to make sure your snowy creation could trick Santa (and Ping-a-Ding). And if snow is a no-go for you, head to the kitchen and gather up some treats instead! Use marshmallows, cookies, or donut holes, plus candies, frosting, peanuts, and other yummy things to create your toy maker look-alike.

Every year, with one week remaining until Christmas Eve, Mrs. Claus hosts a big traditional dinner for everyone at the North Pole. What would you guess is on the menu? Ham, turkey (or both), mashed potatoes and gravy, macaroni and cheese, a casserole of green beans with those strangely delicious crunchy bits sprinkled on top, and some kind of pie topped with ice cream for dessert. Sound about right?

Well, I'll tell you right now. You couldn't be further from the truth.

The traditional North Pole holiday meal is . . . *pizza.* Cheese pizza. Pepperoni pizza. Sausage pizza. Veggie pizza. Mushroom pizza if you're gross. Hawaiian pizza if you want to argue with other elves about the validity of pineapple.

Yup, the Clauses have made pizza their go-to Christmas dinner feast ever since Santa's first worldwide Christmas Eve delivery. On that first trip, Santa and the reindeer were flying over Naples when the man's tummy started to rumble, indicating it was time for a snack break. Now, this was before Santa had become an international celebrity, so he landed the sleigh, squeezed in through the door of a small pizza shop, and ordered a slice. Ever since that moment when the incredible blend of dough, sauce, and cheese passed through his bearded lips, there was no going back. The annual Christmas feast became pizza night.

Now, listen . . . there's a lot I have to say about the way Santa runs things. If I were in charge, elves would not need to make snow twins of themselves to get out of work, no ankles would be bitten, and I'd make peace with those honestly very impressive and good-looking South Pole elves. I'd end the feud with Hank, call off the Scout Elves, and cancel the Naughty List. You know, I think I'd make a pretty terrific Santa! "Elmer Claus, the Elf Who Saved Christmas," they'd call me.

But I will say this about Santa. Every year, he has the Christmas pizzas flown in from Italy, New York, *and* Chicago. The man has excellent taste.

PIZZA PARTY

With supervision, make your own Christmas pizza following this recipe!

❄ Cut a piece of pita bread or a flour tortilla into a Christmassy shape like a snowman, a stocking, or a Christmas tree.

❄ Using a spoon, put a dollop of tomato sauce on it and spread it all around.

❄ Sprinkle mozzarella cheese on top.

❄ Add some toppings, like pepperoni, bacon, veggies, or mushrooms, if you're gross.

❄ Pop your Christmas pizza into a toaster oven until the cheese is all gooey and melted.

❄ Let it cool and then dig in!

THE DAY: DECEMBER 18

Have you ever wondered how the tradition of wearing Ugly Christmas Sweaters during the holiday season came to be? I'm here to tell you that Santa started the trend many years ago.

So when you picture us elves, what do you imagine us wearing? Little green outfits, funny-looking slippers, striped tights, and droopy hats? Well, first of all, that's awfully stereotypical of you. But yeah, that funny green outfit is pretty close to what our uniform is. That is, until December 18.

Beginning on the eighteenth, all elves are required to wear Ugly Christmas Sweaters until December 23, at which point Santa holds the annual Ugly Christmas Sweater Pageant as part of the Eve of Christmas Eve Celebration. And the prize for the winner of the contest? A trip to Cancun. Last year, I actually scored an honorary mention for my red-and-brown striped sweater with a giant, sparkly jalapeño.

Here's what Santa looks for in an Ugly Christmas Sweater:

 If it's not red and green, it had *better* be light blue and brown.

 Three-dimensional elements that pop out, like puffy pom-poms or fake flowers.

 Anything that sparkles, such as tinsel, glitter, sequins, or rhinestones.

 Sweaters featuring animals get bonus points.

PROJECT RUNWAY

Now *you* get to be the judge of the Ugly Christmas Sweater Pageant. Check out the sweaters on the runway. Which sweater do you think will win, based on Santa's guidelines?

BONUS

With permission, turn one of your own sweaters into the ultimate Ugly Christmas Sweater. Remember the things Santa looks for in an ugly sweater and you just might win that trip to Cancun!

I'm sure you've all heard the tale of the grinch that stole Christmas. But what if I told you that *that* story, out of all the Christmas tales you've read is the one that is actually true?

It all started with Santa's estranged brother-in-law Hank, a bucket of green paint, and a poorly thought-out plan.

It was years and years ago that Hank, jealous of Santa's success and adoration, set out on a mission to ruin Santa's good name. He wanted to show the world the truth about the quirky, calculating man he knew Santa to be. So, in order to disguise himself as Santa Claus, he hired a team of professional makeup elves to make him look identical to his rival. What he didn't plan on, though, was tripping and falling into a huge vat of green paint on the way out. His disguise was ruined, he was painted bright green, but he couldn't stop now. He had a mission!

Hank followed his brother-in-law on that fateful Christmas Eve, hitting houses that ol' Saint Nick had just visited and wreaking absolute havoc. He destroyed trees, opened gifts, and tore up children's carefully crafted letters to Santa. He wrote "SANTA WUZ HERE" in green on every house, using his paint-covered fingers. Hank had plans to go to every house after Santa had left it, but here is where the story takes a turn. After just 19 houses, Prancer and Vixen realized that they'd left the vat of Santa's slippery jelly behind.

Santa and the team doubled back, only to spot a dripping green Hank, elbow deep into the word *WUZ*. The police were called and Hank was apprehended before any more damage was done.

It was later that night, after posting bail, that Hank began to cook up his Mall Santa scheme, switching gears from making a mockery of Santa . . . to actually replacing him.

SANTA SCRAMBLE

Why is Hank referred to as a grinch in the story? The truth is, it's an acronym: G.R.I.N.C.H. Unscramble these words that describe Hank and his unforgiveable behaviors. We'll start you off with the first one!

GERDEY   GREEDY   NGUTHAY   _____

REUD   _____   CEPYRE   _____

IMRMTAUE _____   HRELSEAST _____

Now that you know the truth about Santa, it's time to expose the truth about Randolph the Red-Nosed Reindeer. What? Oh, the name. Randy the Reindeer? Renaldo? Reggie? Redman? Rudolfo?

Fine, fine, it's Rudolph. We all know it's Rudolph. His story is iconic. He was bullied for having a blinding red spotlight instead of a nose and then, on a foggy night (that for some unknown reason Santa hadn't prepared for . . . after centuries of working this gig) Rudolph came through and lit the way with that schnoz of his. Sorry if I sound bitter, but the thing is, this guy will not stop telling the story. Rudolph considers himself a local North Pole celebrity. Every chance he gets, with a mug of hot apple cider in his hoof, he'll rope you in and start telling the same old story again. He even hired someone to write a song about it, which he sings every chance he gets. Maybe you've heard of it?

The reality is that Santa doesn't need Rudolph and his nose anymore. It's the twenty-first century! The man has high beam halogen lights on his sleigh, for goodness' sake! Rudolph gets to keep leading the sleigh because he spends the whole year kissing up to Santa. "Hey Santa, is there anything I can do for you?" "If you need a caddy to carry your golf clubs, I'm your deer!" "Here, Santa. Have my slice of sausage and extra cheese. I'm not hungry anymore." "Hey Santa, remember that foggy Christmas Eve? Man, if I hadn't been there, that would've been, like, a *huge* disaster, huh? Anyway, got any idea who's going to lead the way this year?"

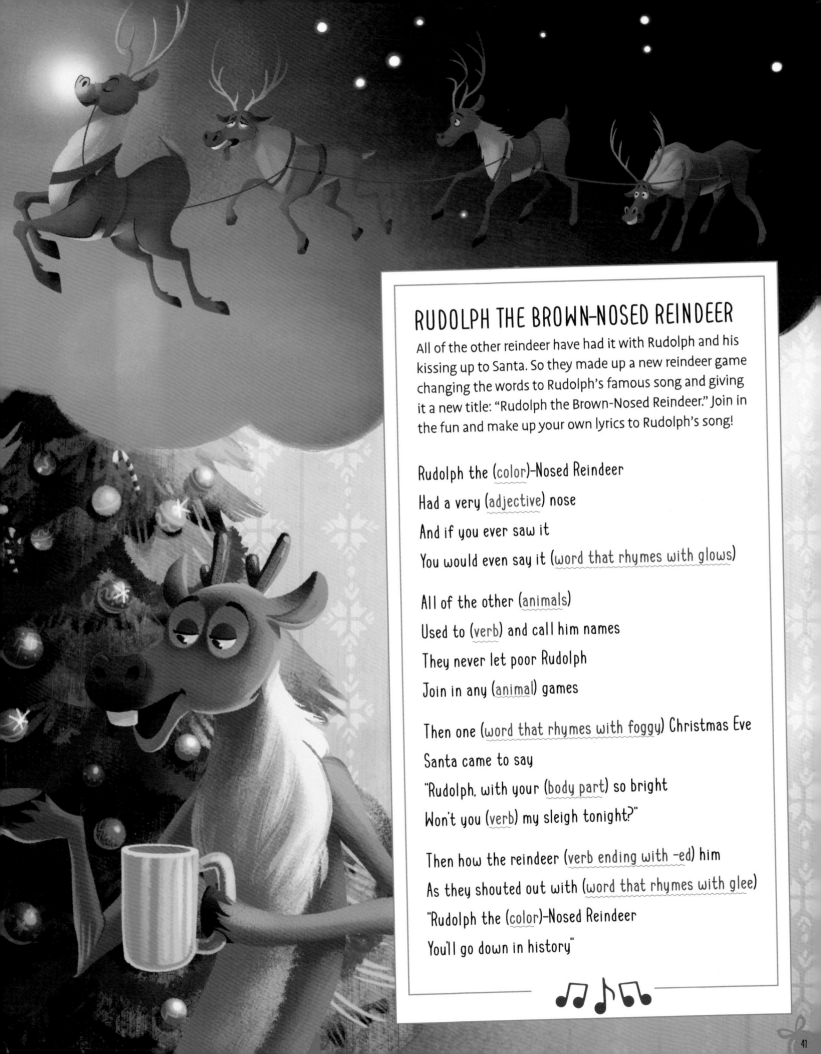

RUDOLPH THE BROWN-NOSED REINDEER

All of the other reindeer have had it with Rudolph and his kissing up to Santa. So they made up a new reindeer game changing the words to Rudolph's famous song and giving it a new title: "Rudolph the Brown-Nosed Reindeer." Join in the fun and make up your own lyrics to Rudolph's song!

Rudolph the (color)-Nosed Reindeer

Had a very (adjective) nose

And if you ever saw it

You would even say it (word that rhymes with glows)

All of the other (animals)

Used to (verb) and call him names

They never let poor Rudolph

Join in any (animal) games

Then one (word that rhymes with foggy) Christmas Eve

Santa came to say

"Rudolph, with your (body part) so bright

Won't you (verb) my sleigh tonight?"

Then how the reindeer (verb ending with -ed) him

As they shouted out with (word that rhymes with glee)

"Rudolph the (color)-Nosed Reindeer

You'll go down in history"

There's one more fact about Santa I must share . . . but I have to warn you. It's a shocker.

The truth is, we elves aren't the only ones with names chosen by something as random as a metallic plate crashing to the floor and the color of a crayon. I mean, let's be honest . . . did you think the man's given name could actually be as simple as Santa Claus? Santa's real name is Tamoshantamis Pinkleclaushensteen.

Yes, I know. It's a mouthful. The family name was given to baby Tam on the day he was born, proudly passed down from a long line of Pinkleclaushensteens.

As Tamoshantamis grew up, he patiently corrected acquaintances, friends, even his own family members as they repeatedly mispronounced his name. And later, when Operation Christmas was up and running, he endured all the horrible misspellings on letters addressed to him. Finally one day, Tam's head Screener Elf came to him with a solution: why not eliminate a bunch of those pesky letters, shortening the name to SANTA CLAUS? And the rest, as they say, is history.

But what about those other names Santa's known by?

Saint Nick? Santa loves the idea of being considered a saint, but the truth is, he has no idea who "Nick" is.

Babbo Natale? Fun to say for sure, but that's actually the nickname the Italians gave Santa after his first visit to the little Italian pizzeria on the corner.

Kris Kringle? Santa came up with that on Carnival Night one year, spinning the wheel of Christmassy-Sounding Names.

And if you think Pinkleclaushensteen is hard to say, try Weihnachtsmann, which is what kids in Germany call the Big Man in Red.

So now you understand why, when Tamoshantamis P. finally changed his name to Santa Claus, we all breathed a sigh of relief.

NAME-CHANGER

It's Carnival Night! Play Santa's random name-generating games to find your own Christmassy-sounding name!

FIRST NAME = Your birth month
LAST NAME = The first letter of your first name

JANUARY	GUMDROP
FEBRUARY	PEPPERMINT
MARCH	COCOA
APRIL	SNOWFLAKE
MAY	CINNAMON
JUNE	FIGGY
JULY	TWINKLE
AUGUST	JELLY BEAN
SEPTEMBER	SUGARPLUM
OCTOBER	PUDDING
NOVEMBER	GINGERBREAD
DECEMBER	MARSHMALLOW

A - Angelbottoms
B - Buttonbells
C - Cracklekins
D - Dashalot
E - Eggnogamous
F - Frostycakes
G - Gingerpants
H - Happybeard
I - Ice Creamsicles
J - Jingledash
K - Kringlemas
L - Logbottom
M - McJingles
N - Naughtykins
O - O'Mistleytoes
P - Pinkleclaushensteen
Q - Quicksprinkles
R - Ribboncakes
S - Sparklepants
T - Tinseltoes
U - Ugly Sweater
V - Van Jinglepotts
W - Winterbottoms
X - X-Mas
Y - Yumbuttons
Z - Zippykins

THE DAY: DECEMBER 22

Many children wonder what happens if you *don't* fall asleep on Christmas Eve. What if the excitement overcomes you and you cannot drift into slumber? What if, as you lay awake in bed, you hear Santa being pushed down your not-exactly-Santa-friendly chimney by Prancer and Vixen. You may hear, "Ow! Take it easy!" or "Enough with the jelly, already! I'm covered in the stuff!"

What would happen, for instance, if you were to catch a glimpse of Santa in action?

That, my friend, is a job for the Coal Patrol.

As soon as a snooping child is caught attempting to pull off a Santa sighting, two things happen.

First, as you know, Dancer will come to your window and utter her startling bray to send you scurrying back to bed. Then, the Scout Elf waiting on your shelf will alert Santa to abort the mission. Santa will pop back into the chimney and escape, taking all of those gifts with him that were originally intended for you.

Subsequently, the Coal Patrol, a squad of Special Agent Elves, arrives in their coal-dust-powered sleigh to leave you a charred, nasty nugget in place of that present you had your little heart set on. Yup, it's a cold, coal world out there, kids.

LOOK & FIND

Hidden in this living room are 12 pieces of coal. Can you find all 12? If so, maybe the Coal Patrol will cut you some slack this year!

You may be wondering if Santa really drinks all that milk and eats all those cookies you leave out on Christmas Eve.

The short answer is no, but there's more to it than that. I know I've spent a lot of time exposing the reality about Santa, you know, stickin' it to the man . . . but the truth is maybe a bit more, uh . . . *complicated*. I was going to write that Santa doesn't care about your cookies. I was even going to tell you about a conversation I overheard Santa having with an elf on the Coal Patrol. "Snickerdoodles again?" he complained. "I've got the biggest craving for a pineapple upside-down cake and some sparkling apple cider. But what do I get every time? Cookies and milk. It's coal time for this kid!"

But that's a lie. The truth is, ever since the one year when Santa ate every cookie on every plate at every house and gained 97 pounds, Mrs. Claus has forbidden him from eating them. It wasn't even that Santa wanted the cookies. He was still full from all the pizza. The way Santa tells it, he just didn't want to hurt the feelings of the kids who had left those cookies out for him.

So now, after Santa collects the cookies, he gives them to the Cookie Redistribution Elves to deliver, while still fresh, to charitable organizations. The only sweets Mrs. Claus can't keep Santa from eating are his favorite chocolate chip cinna-spice cookies that his own mother used to make when he was a little boy.

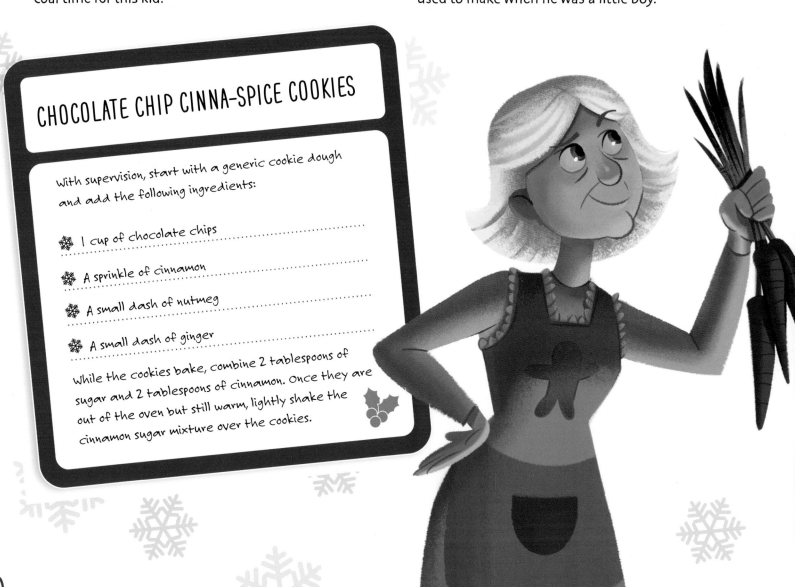

CHOCOLATE CHIP CINNA-SPICE COOKIES

With supervision, start with a generic cookie dough and add the following ingredients:

❄ 1 cup of chocolate chips

❄ A sprinkle of cinnamon

❄ A small dash of nutmeg

❄ A small dash of ginger

While the cookies bake, combine 2 tablespoons of sugar and 2 tablespoons of cinnamon. Once they are out of the oven but still warm, lightly shake the cinnamon sugar mixture over the cookies.

I wrote this book to expose the truth about Christmas magic, Santa, the elves, and all the rest . . . but the holiday spirit has gotten to me. I have a confession to make. My name is Elmer Elffenstock. My code name is Splat Brown. I am a South Pole elf and a double agent for Hank. The plan was to write a tell-all as an overworked, underappreciated North Pole elf. And once the Claus was cancelled, Hank and the South Pole elves would replace Christmas . . . with Hankmas.

But as I spent time at the North Pole, I noticed Santa's decency. Remember that story about how I was chased by Noel the Attack Penguin? Santa actually saved me and, instead of trusting Noel's instincts that I was a South Pole elf, he helped me care for my beak-wounds. And the whole overworked elf thing? Untrue.

Hank and the South Pole elves believe Santa is a fraud. But all I've seen during my time with him is kindness and Christmas magic.

He's everything you want him to be and more. He doesn't punish children for being naughty, just like he doesn't reward elves that suck up to him and punish those of us who . . . you know, build snow clones or go on stamp rampages. (Shoutout to Speeeerang!) Instead, Santa treats all of us like family.

So I've made a decision. Once Santa returns from his Christmas Eve deliveries, I'm going to confess. I will tell him that the Christmas spirit has inspired me to change my ways . . . and my holiday wish will be for Santa to give me a second chance.

If I can expose one final truth about Christmas, let it be this: The best gift you can give yourself is finding and cherishing the goodness in others.

Merry Christmas!

SHARE THE MAGIC
Christmas is about the magic of being together. Spend time with your family and friends, sharing your wishes and dreams for yourselves and each other this Christmas.

INSIGHT
KIDS

PO Box 3088
San Rafael, CA 94912

f www.insighteditions.com

y Find us on Facebook: www.facebook.com/InsightEditions
Follow us on Twitter: @insighteditions

Library of Congress Cataloging-in-Publication Data available.

ISBN: 978-1-64722-451-6

Publisher: Raoul Goff
VP of Licensing and Partnerships: Vanessa Lopez
VP of Creative: Chrissy Kwasnik
VP of Manufacturing: Alix Nicholaeff
Associate Publisher: Sara Miller
Art Director: Stuart Smith
Editorial Assistant: Elizabeth Ovieda
Managing Editor: Vicki Jaeger
Senior Production Editor: Jennifer Bentham
Senior Production Manager: Greg Steffen
Senior Production Manager, Subsidiary Rights: Lina s Palma

Insight Editions, in association with Roots of Peace, will plant two trees for each tree
used in the manufacturing of this book. Roots of Peace is an internationally renowned
humanitarian organization dedicated to eradicating land mines worldwide and converting
war-torn lands into productive farms and wildlife habitats. Roots of Peace will plant two
million fruit and nut trees in Afghanistan and provide farmers there with the skills and
support necessary for sustainable land use.

Manufactured in China by Insight Editions

10 9 8 7 6 5 4 3 2 1